11.22

W0007550

SPORTS

VIP s

MEET
TOM BRADY

JOE LEVIT

SPORTS THRILLS
MEET
RESEARCH SKILLS

Lerner SPORTS

Free Database Trial: **lernersports.com**

To Tom Jacobs, who I'm sure will love reading this!

Lerner Publications Company
An imprint of Lerner Publishing Group, Inc.
241 First Avenue North
Minneapolis, MN 55401 USA

For reading levels and more information, look up this title at www.lernerbooks.com.

Main body text set in Aptifer Slab LT Pro. Typeface provided by Linotype AG.

Library of Congress Cataloging-in-Publication Data

Names: Levit, Joseph, author.
Title: Meet Tom Brady / Joe Levit.
Description: Minneapolis: Lerner Publications, 2023. | Series: Sports VIPs | Includes bibliographical references and index. | Audience: Ages 7–11 | Audience: Grades 2–3 | Summary: "Quarterback Tom Brady set a record by winning six Super Bowls with the New England Patriots. In 2021, he led the Tampa Bay Buccaneers to the title. Explore his life on and off the field"—Provided by publisher.
Identifiers: LCCN 2021043430 (print) | LCCN 2021043431 (ebook) | ISBN 9781728458168 (library binding) | ISBN 9781728463353 (paperback) | ISBN 9781728462332 (ebook)
Subjects: LCSH: Brady, Tom, 1977-–Juvenile literature. | Quarterbacks (Football)—United States—Biography—Juvenile literature.
Classification: LCC GV939.B685 L48 2023 (print) | LCC GV939.B685 (ebook) | DDC 796.332092 [B]—dc23

LC record available at https://lccn.loc.gov/2021043430
LC ebook record available at https://lccn.loc.gov/2021043431

Manufactured in the United States of America
1-50846-50183-12/6/2021

TABLE OF CONTENTS

>>>>>>>>>>>>>>>>>>>>

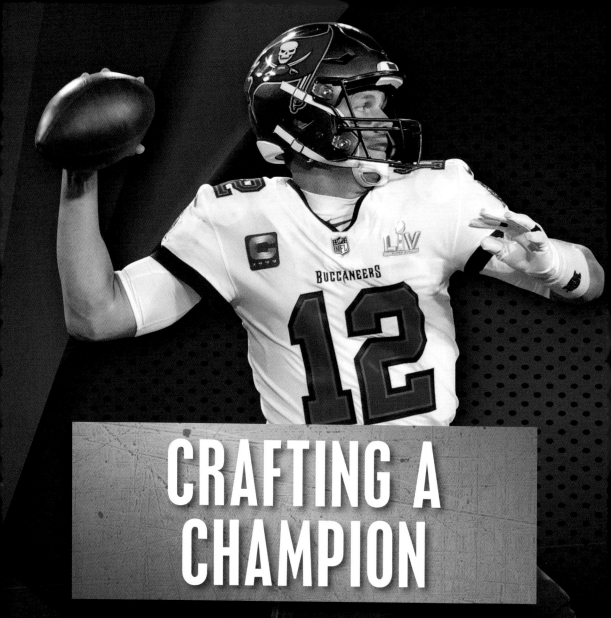

CRAFTING A CHAMPION

Sometimes, all it takes is one great player. That's what Tampa Bay Buccaneers head coach Bruce Arians thought in 2020. His team had plenty of talent. But it lacked a strong quarterback.

Luckily for Arians, superstar quarterback Tom Brady became a free agent for the first time that year. To the surprise of many fans, Arians convinced Brady to join the Buccaneers. "You can't hit a home run if you don't swing for one," said Arians.

FAST FACTS

DATE OF BIRTH: August 3, 1977
POSITION: quarterback
LEAGUE: National Football League (NFL)

PROFESSIONAL HIGHLIGHTS: has won the Super Bowl seven times; set a record by playing in the playoffs for 12 straight seasons; at 40, became the oldest player to win the NFL Most Valuable Player (MVP) award

PERSONAL HIGHLIGHTS: grew up playing football, basketball, and baseball in San Mateo, California; has three children, Jack, Benjamin, and Vivian; has hosted *Saturday Night Live*

Coach Arians and Brady talk about the next play.

Tampa Bay had a strong 11–5 record in 2020. Brady really got rolling once the playoffs started. He and the Buccaneers played three straight playoff games against Super Bowl–winning quarterbacks. First he beat Drew Brees and the New Orleans Saints. Then he topped the Green Bay Packers led by quarterback Aaron Rodgers. In the Super Bowl, the Buccaneers faced Patrick Mahomes and the Kansas City Chiefs.

The Chiefs were one of the most exciting teams in the NFL. They had won the Super Bowl the year before with Mahomes leading the way. But they were no match for Brady and the Buccaneers. Tampa Bay scored three touchdowns in the first half. They added 10 more points in the second half to win 31–9.

Brady threw three touchdowns in the game. He won the Super Bowl MVP award for a record-setting fifth time. He had proven once again that he was the greatest quarterback of all time.

Brady completed 21 of 29 pass attempts during the 2021 Super Bowl.

CHAPTER 1

A LOVE OF THE GAME

Tom loved football from the start. He played touch and flag football in elementary school in San Mateo, California. Along with the rest of his family, Tom was a fan of the San Francisco 49ers.

Tom was in the stands at Candlestick Park in San Francisco, California, for the 1981 National Football Conference championship game. His hero was San Francisco quarterback Joe Montana. Tom saw Montana complete an amazing touchdown pass to Dwight Clark. Fans called it "The Catch." The great play helped the 49ers beat the Dallas Cowboys 28–27.

In 1995, Tom (*back row, second from right*) played on a high school baseball all-star team. He also played football and basketball at Junipero Serra High School.

In ninth grade, Tom wrote about his future plans: "One day, I'm going to be a household name." He wanted to be a famous athlete. But he had a long way to go to reach his dream.

As a high school freshman, Tom played backup quarterback on a losing team. When the starter got hurt, Tom took over. But the team didn't win a game all season.

In 1996, Brady started playing football at the University of Michigan. He was a backup quarterback in his first two seasons. The starter was Brian Griese, son of

Brady gets ready to throw a pass during a Michigan practice.

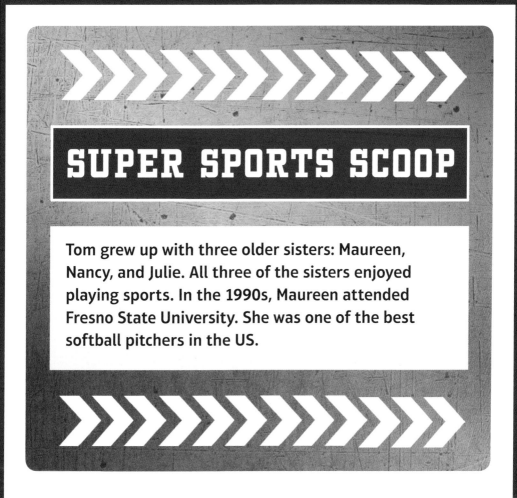

NFL quarterback Bob Griese. In 1997, Brian Griese led the Michigan Wolverines to share the national championship with the University of Nebraska. Brady hoped to reach such heights on his own.

The next season, Michigan brought in Drew Henson to play quarterback. Brady had to compete against Henson for playing time. That forced Brady to excel when he was on the field. He threw 14 touchdown passes in 1998 and 16 in 1999.

Brady warms up before a Patriots game in 2000.

Despite playing part-time in college, Brady proved that he could win football games. But at the 2000 NFL Draft, teams chose six quarterbacks before him. Brady had expected a team to pick him in the second or third round. Instead, the New England Patriots chose him in the sixth round.

Brady was upset that so many teams had overlooked his skills and passed on him in the draft. But he remained confident and was thrilled to join the NFL. After the draft, he spoke with Patriots owner Robert Kraft. Brady told Kraft, "You'll never regret picking me." Brady was ready to prove his bold words.

Robert Kraft has owned the Patriots since 1994.

CHAPTER 2

EARLY SUCCESS

Brady started his NFL career as a backup quarterback. Drew Bledsoe (*pictured above*) was the Patriots starter. But in the second game of the 2001 season, Bledsoe took a huge hit from a New York Jets defender. The quarterback injured his chest and missed the rest of the season. Brady took over and guided the Patriots to 11 wins in 14 games. That included a six-game winning streak to end the season.

In the first game of the 2001 playoffs, the Patriots got lucky. They were down 13–10 against the Oakland Raiders. With less than two minutes left, Oakland defender Charles Woodson tackled Brady and knocked the ball loose. The Raiders jumped on it. But the referees said Brady's hand was moving forward when he lost the ball. They changed the play to an incomplete pass. The Patriots kept possession of the ball and kicked a field goal to tie the score. In overtime, they kicked another field goal to win the game 16–13.

Since joining the NFL, Brady has spent a lot of time helping his community. Here he meets with kids during an event with Best Buddies International.

Brady throws a pass during the 2002 Super Bowl. The victory was the first Super Bowl win in team history.

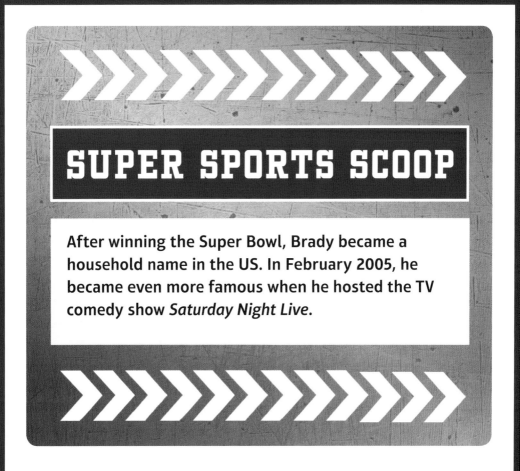

The Patriots beat the Pittsburgh Steelers next. Then they faced the St. Louis Rams in the Super Bowl. Brady became the youngest quarterback ever to win the big game in a tight 20–17 victory.

The next season, the Patriots went 9–7 and failed to make the playoffs. But they began a dynasty in 2003 and 2004. The Patriots had 14–2 records and went on to win the Super Bowl both years. With Brady at quarterback, the Patriots were destined for greatness.

CHAPTER 3

ALMOST PERFECT

In 2005 and 2006, the Patriots lost in the playoffs. The 2006 loss was to Brady's rival, Indianapolis Colts quarterback Peyton Manning. The Patriots led the game 21–6 at halftime. But the Colts came back to win 38–34.

After the loss, the Patriots looked for ways to improve. In 2007, the team traded for top wide receiver Randy Moss. With Moss and Brady, the season became one for the ages. The two superstars overran the NFL. Brady threw 50 touchdown passes to break Manning's single-season record.

Randy Moss catches a touchdown pass. Moss set a record in 2007 with 23 touchdown catches in 16 games.

The Patriots won all of their regular-season games in 2007. The team had a chance to complete the first 19–0 season in NFL history. But in the Super Bowl, the New York Giants stuffed Brady and the Patriots 17–14.

After the loss, Brady's life changed on and off the field. He injured his knee in the first game of the 2008 season and missed the rest of the year. In 2009, he married famous fashion model Gisele Bündchen.

SUPER SPORTS SCOOP

Brady's son Jack was born in 2007 to model and actor Bridget Moynahan. Brady and Bündchen's son, Benjamin, was born in 2009. Their daughter, Vivian, was born in 2012.

Brady throws the ball just before a Giants defender crashes into him during the 2012 Super Bowl.

Brady's knee healed, and he was back on the field for the 2009 season. In one game, he set an NFL record by throwing five touchdowns in one quarter! The next season, Brady broke Brett Favre's record for most home wins in a row with 26. The Patriots made it back to the Super Bowl in 2012. But once again, the Giants beat them. This time, New England lost 21–17.

CHAPTER 4

LATE-CAREER HEROICS

Brady works hard to stay strong and healthy. He stretches and exercises to remain flexible and avoid injuries. He works with experts to improve his throwing and get ready for games.

Brady also spends time with his business and charity interests. In 2013, he helped start a company. TB12 helps athletes improve and recover from injuries with workouts, healthful food, and other programs.

Paying attention to his body and his diet is a way of life for Brady. His meals are mostly fruits, vegetables, and grains. He also eats meat like fish and chicken. But sometimes Brady eats something just because it tastes good. Cheeseburgers are one of his favorite foods.

TB12 products are designed to help people live healthful lives.

Thanks to his success in football, business, and entertainment, Brady is one of the most famous athletes in the world.

At the end of the 2014 season, Brady and the Patriots met the Seattle Seahawks in the Super Bowl. The Seahawks had destroyed Peyton Manning and his new team, the Denver Broncos, in the previous Super Bowl. Seattle was a tough opponent.

The Seahawks led the Patriots by 10 points at the end of the third quarter. But Brady threw two touchdown passes in the fourth quarter. The Patriots won 28–24. The comeback was the largest in Super Bowl history at the time.

Two seasons later, Brady and his teammates reached the Super Bowl yet again. This time, they faced the Atlanta Falcons. The Falcons took it to the Patriots early. Atlanta led 21–0 in the first half.

On the sideline, Falcons receiver Mohamed Sanu said that Brady had never faced such a tough attack. Teammate Taylor Gabriel wasn't so confident. "It's Tom Brady though," Gabriel said. He knew that Brady had the skill to lead New England to a comeback.

In the second half, the Patriots fell even further behind. With the score 28–3, the team began to play much better. Brady threw two touchdown passes to help the Patriots tie the game. In overtime, a James White scoring run sealed the 34–28 victory for New England. Brady

Brady zips a pass to an open teammate in the 2017 Super Bowl. He led New England to 25 second-half points against the Falcons.

broke his own record by leading the Patriots to the largest comeback in Super Bowl history.

In 2017, Brady won his third NFL MVP award. At 40, he was the oldest player to win the award. His great play helped the Patriots reach another Super Bowl. But this time, they lost to the Philadelphia Eagles 41–33. A year later, Brady led his team to a 13–3 Super Bowl win over the Los Angeles Rams.

With seven Super Bowl wins, Brady has a reputation among many as the best football player ever. "I played with one of the best quarterbacks of all time in Peyton

Brady holds his daughter during a boat parade in 2021 to celebrate Tampa Bay's Super Bowl win.

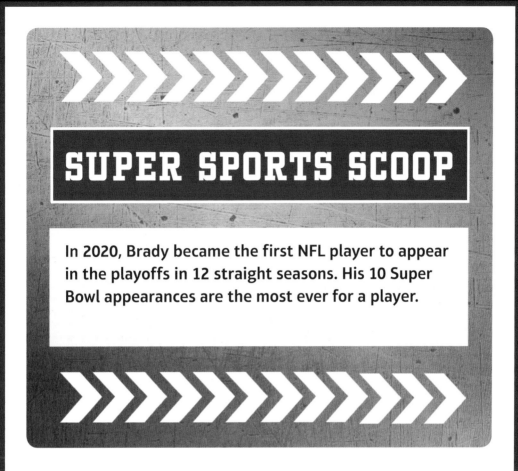

Manning," said former Colts wide receiver Reggie Wayne. "It's hard for me to say this, but it's true: Tom Brady is the best of all time." With Brady's focus on health and fitness, he could keep playing and winning for a long time to come.

TOM BRADY
CAREER STATS

GAMES STARTED:

316

PASSES ATTEMPTED:

11,317

PASSES COMPLETED:

7,263

PASSING TOUCHDOWNS:

624

PASSING YARDS:

84,520

INTERCEPTIONS:

203

GLOSSARY

backup: a person who takes the place of or supports another

comeback: to recover after being behind in a game or contest

draft: when teams take turns choosing new players

dynasty: a team that is very successful for a long time

flexible: easy to move and bend

free agent: a player who is free to join any team

household name: a person or thing whose name is very well known

overtime: extra time added to a game when the score is tied at the end of the normal playing time

rival: a player or team that tries to defeat or be more successful than another

starter: a player in the lineup at the beginning of a game

wide receiver: a football player whose main job is to catch passes

SOURCE NOTES

5   Dan Lyons, "Bruce Arians Sums Up the Buccaneer's Pursuit of Tom Brady," Spun, January 28, 2021, https://thespun.com /nfl/nfc-south/tampa-bay-buccaneers/tom-brady-tampa -bay-buccaneers-bruce-arians-quote-home-run-super -bowl#:~:text=%23GoBucs%20coach%20Bruce%20Arians%20 on,or%20have%20some%20damn%20fun.

10 Rich Cimini, "Story of Boy Named Tom Brady," *New York Daily News*, January 25, 2008, https://www.nydailynews.com /sports/football/giants/story-boy-named-tom-brady-article -1.341686.

13 "Tom Brady Dispels a Great Patriots Myth about Post-Draft Message to Robert Kraft," WBZ, April 8, 2020, https://boston .cbslocal.com/2020/04/08/tom-brady-dispels-a-great-patriots -myth-about-post-draft-message-to-robert-kraft/.

25 Andrew Joseph, "One Falcons Player Sensed the Tom Brady Comeback, but No One Listened to Him," For the Win, February 8, 2017, https://ftw.usatoday.com/2017/02/falcons -player-taylor-gabriel-micd-up-warned-tom-brady-super -bowl-comeback-video-nfl.

26-27 Michael David Smith, "Tom Brady's Greatness, in the Words of His Fellow Greats," Yahoo!, February 2, 2019, https://www .yahoo.com/now/tom-brady-greatness-words-fellow -123329351.html.

LEARN MORE

Frederickson, Kevin. *Tom Brady.* Minnetonka, MN: Kaleidoscope, 2020.

Hill, Christina. *Inside the New England Patriots.* Minneapolis: Lerner Publications, 2023.

Levit, Joe. *Football's G.O.A.T.: Jim Brown, Tom Brady, and More.* Minneapolis: Lerner Publications, 2020.

National Football League
https://www.nfl.com

Tampa Bay Buccaneers
https://www.buccaneers.com

TB12 Foundation
https://tb12foundation.org

INDEX

PHOTO ACKNOWLEDGMENTS

Image credits: REUTERS/Brian Snyder/Alamy Stock Photo, p. 4; Cliff Welch/Icon Sportswire/Getty Images, p. 6; AP Photo/Jason Behnken, p. 7; AP Photo/Don Montague, p. 8; MediaNews Group/The Mercury News via Getty Images, p. 9; AP Photo/Scott Audette, p. 10; AP Photo/Al Messerschmidt, p. 12; AP Photo/Kathy Willens, p. 13; Jonathan Daniel/Allsport/Getty Images, p. 14; Paul Marotta/Getty Images for Best Buddies, p. 15; AP Photo/Tom DiPace, p. 16; Matthew West/MediaNews Group/Boston Herald via Getty Images, p. 18; Rhona Wise/Bloomberg via Getty Images, p. 19; Mark Cornelison/Lexington Herald-Leader/Tribune News Service via Getty Images, p. 21; Mike Ehrmann/Getty Images, p. 22; John Tlumacki/The Boston Globe via Getty Images, p. 23; Nic Antaya for The Boston Globe via Getty Images, p. 24; Bob Levey/Getty Images, p. 25; AP Photo/Phelan M. Ebenhack, p. 26. Design elements: The Hornbills Studio/Shutterstock.com; Tamjaii9/Shutterstock.com.

Cover: AP Photo/Mark LoMoglio.